That Special Starry Night

The Christmas Story

retold and illustrated by Jeff Carnehl

CPH
Concordia Publishing House

On a chilly December night the wind swirled around freshly made snowmen. Inside, the home was cozy and warm, filled with the sweet smells and sounds of Christmas. As the children hung their favorite ornaments on the tree, Dad said, "Let me tell you the story of what happened on a special starry night."

Over 2,000 years ago, Caesar Augustus ordered all the people in the Roman empire to be counted. Everyone was to travel to the birthplace of their family.

So Joseph traveled to Bethlehem because King David was his ancestor. He took Mary with him for they were pledged to be married. Mary was expecting a baby who would be born very soon.

When Mary and Joseph finally reached Bethlehem, they were both very tired. But every inn, or hotel, was filled. There was not even one empty room in the whole town.

NO ROOM

Finally, they found a stable where they could stay. And on that night, my favorite starry night, the baby was born. Mary carefully wrapped the baby in cloths and placed Him in a manger filled with warm straw.

Meanwhile, in the grassy fields outside Bethlehem, there were shepherds watching over their flocks of sheep.

All of a sudden, an angel appeared to the shepherds and said, "Don't be afraid. I have happy news for you. Tonight a Savior has been born for you and all people. His name is Jesus. You will find Him wrapped in cloths, lying in a manger."

Suddenly, the shepherds saw many more angels singing praises to God. The angels were saying, "Glory to God in the highest, and peace to all people on earth!"

After the angels had left them and gone back to heaven, the shepherds said to one another, "Let's go to Bethlehem and see for ourselves what God has told us!"

So the shepherds hurried away to Bethlehem. They couldn't wait to see the newborn Savior.

When the shepherds arrived, they found the stable. Inside they saw Mary, and Joseph, and the baby who was lying in the manger—just as the angel had said.

The shepherds were so excited! They rushed away to tell everyone about the baby, the newborn Savior. Then the shepherds returned to their flocks, rejoicing and singing praises to God for the things they had seen and heard.

Dad stopped to gaze at the twinkling Christmas tree. He asked his family, "Who can *you* tell about Jesus' birth on that special starry night?"

And everyone smiled.

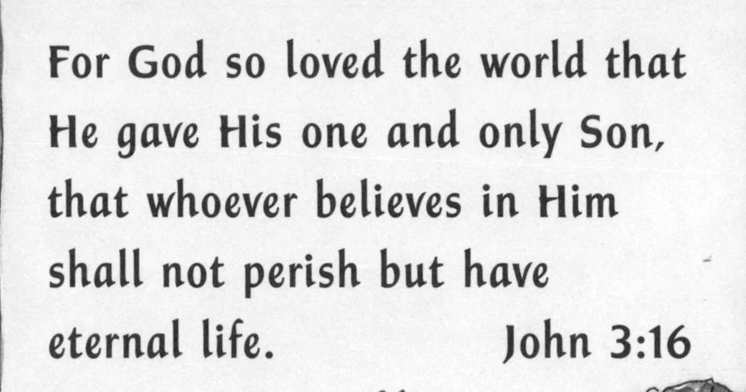

You can find the story of the Savior's birth in Luke 2:1–20.